THE VILLAGE
BASKET WEAVER

The VILLAGE BASKET WEAVER

by JONATHAN LONDON

illustrated by GEORGE CRESPO

DUTTON CHILDREN'S BOOKS ◆ NEW YORK

FOR THE PEOPLE OF HOPKINS, BELIZE,
WITH ADMIRATION AND GRATITUDE
J.L.

FOR CLAUDETTE AND FOR ALL THE PEOPLE OF THE CARIB TERRITORY
IN THE COMMONWEALTH OF DOMINICA
G.C.

Text copyright © 1996 by Jonathan London
Illustrations copyright © 1996 by George Crespo
All rights reserved.
CIP Data is available.
Published in the United States 1996 by Dutton Children's Books,
a division of Penguin Books USA Inc.
375 Hudson Street, New York, New York 10014
Designed by Semadar Megged
Printed in Hong Kong
First Edition
ISBN 0-525-45314-8
1 3 5 7 9 10 8 6 4 2

Except for the fishermen, Tavio was almost the first one awake in the village. He couldn't wait to see his grandfather, Policarpio, who rose at dawn to sit at his work beneath the cashew tree near the beach.

Policarpio, or Carpio, as most people called him, was the village basket weaver. He was old, old—Tavio didn't know how old. Old like the ancient sea turtles who crawled out of the waves to bury their eggs in the sand. Old like the wrinkled sea itself.

Tavio scampered down the steps of his house and ran toward the long beach, dribbling a coconut like a soccer ball with his bare feet.

"Grandfather!"

"Good morning, Grandchild," said Policarpio, his hands not pausing from their work. It seemed to Tavio that everything about his grandfather was woven into the baskets: his silences and his strength, the smoky smell from his corncob pipe, the salty smell of the sea.

"What kind of basket are you making today?" the boy asked, flopping down on the ground.

"Ah, my little monkey," said the basket weaver, pushing a slender strand into the weave with his fingers. "You are always so curious. That's good. This, Tavio, will be the basket used by the whole village for the making of cassava bread. Soon it will be as tall as a man."

"But what's the matter with the old one?" asked Tavio.

"When things get old," sighed Carpio, "they get tired and weak, just like people."

"You're old," said Tavio, "but you're not tired and weak. Are you?"

Carpio was silent for a moment. With a soft smile, he leaned forward into his work.

"Yes, Tavio, I am tired," said Carpio. "And weak. But I am the only person in the village who remembers how to make a cassava basket. I must do this one last thing. Then, perhaps, I can rest."

Like his grandfather, Tavio was as skinny as a monkey. But he wasn't weak. He made a muscle and felt it. Then he looked at his grandfather, and for the first time he noticed how the muscles and veins in Carpio's long thin arms twined and twisted, like strands woven into a basket.

The sun was already warm on Tavio's shoulders. It was time for him to go home for breakfast. There he ate his johnnycakes, then walked slowly down the beach to the village school, hands deep in his hip pockets.

During his lessons, as the teacher tapped her pointer on the numbers filling the blackboard, Tavio gazed out the window. A tall, lone palm leaned like a man bent over the beach. Like an old man.

Like his grandfather, Carpio.

Tavio was so worried about Carpio that he couldn't pay attention to his teacher or his work.

After he got home from school, Tavio went to watch the women who were making bread out of cassava. Twice a week, on Tuesdays and Fridays, they worked beneath a thatched roof held up by four posts and made enough bread to feed the whole village.

The women grated the cassava roots into fine pieces, then strained them through the long, cylindrical basket. The cassava squeezer hung freely from a rafter with a weight attached to it at the bottom. As more and more pulp was added, the basket stretched toward the ground. Its woven mesh tightened and squeezed out the poisonous cassava juices. Then the good pulp left behind would be sifted and made into flour. Next the bread would be shaped and baked. Some loaves would be eaten right away; others would be dried and stored.

Tavio's neighbor, Lucia, said, "For you, my friend" as she sliced two pieces from a warm, new batch. Tavio grinned and took a bite of the good, fresh bread.

But yes, Tavio thought, the basket did look old and tired. How much longer would it last?

Early the next morning, Tavio watched as his grandfather wove more of the new cassava basket with his tough, bent fingers.

"There are so few left to carry on the old ways," Carpio was saying. "Now the children grow up and want to move to Belize City. Or maybe they choose to work for the companies that cut down the trees in the forest. They drive big machines…."

Tavio nodded. Like the other children of the village, he often imagined what it would be like to operate a huge Caterpillar tractor or to speed through the jungle in a four-wheel-drive Jeep.

"When I was a boy," Carpio continued, "children learned from their elders how to fish…how to grow bananas and sugarcane and cassava and corn… how to hunt wild peccary and collect honey…how to do the dances and sing the old songs…how to make baskets…"

From that day on, Tavio woke to the rooster's call every morning and slipped out silently to be with his grandfather. Sometimes, if he was early enough, they would stroll the beach together, inspecting shells, listening to the *shush* of pebbles rolling with the drag of waves. Tavio would turn cartwheels, or scuttle sideways like a crab, to make Carpio laugh.

Back under the cashew tree, Carpio would let Tavio sip some coffee, or he would chop a piece of sugarcane for Tavio to chew. Then Carpio told stories while he worked.

Tavio noticed how his grandfather would split the long river reeds for the basket lengthwise, into four pieces each, and then allow them to dry in the sun. He watched carefully as Carpio scraped the dried reeds with a small, sharp knife, fashioning them into long, curving slivers that could be blackened with mud or dyed different colors. Carpio was weaving a beautiful pattern with the colored reeds he made.

Soon Tavio began to play with some broken strands that had been cast aside. Looking up now and then to watch the cassava squeezer grow beneath his grandfather's shaking hands, Tavio began to mold a small basket of his own.

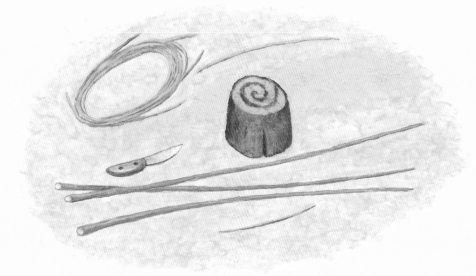

Then one morning, at the pink of dawn, Tavio arrived and found that his grandfather's place beneath the cashew tree was empty. The brine barrel that Carpio used as a seat was still there, and so was the squeezer. It was almost finished now, standing—as his grandfather had said it would—as tall as a man.

Sendio, Tavio's uncle, climbed down the rickety stairs from the one-room house that he shared with his father.

"I knew you'd come, little monkey."

"But where's Grandfather?" asked Tavio.

"Hush, boy," said his uncle, placing a large hand on Tavio's shoulder. "Come with me. We'll talk on the boat."

The sun shone like a pearl in the rosy mist. Sendio rowed out through the surf, then tied fishing lines to each of his toes. He baited triple hooks at the end of each line and dropped them overboard. Finally the fisherman said, "Your grandfather has not many days left. He is very old, and he is dying."

Tavio couldn't speak. Gulls screamed overhead. Dolphins rolled by, but Tavio could see only his grandfather, bent over his baskets, smoking his pipe.

"So no more basket weaving for my father," said Sendio. "It is time for him to rest." Sendio fell silent. The only sound was the *clop-clop* of waves against the hull.

Tavio's eyes burned with salty water, as if the sea had risen inside him and filled them.

Later that day, when school had ended, Tavio ran toward the long beach, his heart pounding as fast as his feet. He found his grandfather once again beneath the cashew tree. But Carpio was not sitting in his place, on the brine barrel where he made his baskets. Instead, the old man was lying in a hammock that had been hung between his cashew tree and a palm.

Tavio stood at Carpio's side. He was breathless from running.

Carpio looked up and grinned. "Grandchild, I have no teeth to eat the cashews or coconut. My eyes are good only to tell shadows from the light. But my mind is clear. I know I must finish this one last thing." He pointed toward the basket, then sighed. "And I'm afraid I cannot."

Tavio was silent for a moment. And in that moment, he made a decision.

"Grandfather!" he said. "I know—tell me how to finish the basket, and I will help you."

Carpio nodded, pleased. It had been his secret wish. He asked for his pipe, then began to whisper instructions. It was like the whispering of the sea. Carpio's words wove a kind of spell around Tavio, who now did as his grandfather told him and thought of nothing else.

And by the time the sun reached the tops of the banana trees growing behind the village, and the day was almost done, the cassava basket was completed. When Carpio saw the finished work, a smile spread across his face, and his eyes closed.

The next day was Friday. It was time again for the women to make cassava bread for the whole village. And for the first time, they used Policarpio's new basket. The soft sea wind carried the sound of their laughter and singing to where he lay and woke him.

When the first slice of the crisp bread was cut, Lucia handed it to Tavio, who ran with it to his grandfather's side.

"Someday, Grandchild," said Policarpio, placing his hand on Tavio's head, "you will make many more things of value."

Eyes shining, Tavio took a bite of the warm bread. It's true, he thought. Who else knows how to make the baskets used by the whole village for the making of cassava bread?

Like his grandfather before him, he would become the village basket weaver.

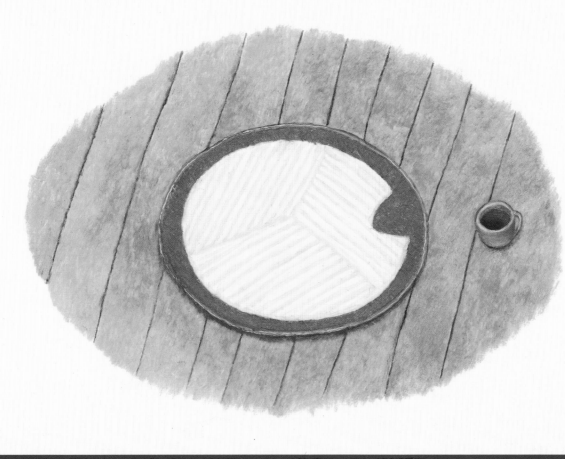

AUTHOR'S NOTE

The Garifuna people of this story, otherwise known as Black Caribs, live along the Caribbean coast of Central America. They are descendants of the island Carib people and Africans who originally inhabited the island of Saint Vincent in the Lesser Antilles. Carib people continue to inhabit an area of Saint Vincent as well as other parts of the Lesser Antilles.

The Garifuna people still speak the Carib language, and in Belize—formerly called British Honduras—most also speak Spanish and English. Many in the small fishing villages feel that their old ways are threatened and encourage their young ones to learn what it means to be Garifuna. I had the good fortune to be invited to live with a Garifuna family in the village of Hopkins on the coast of Belize. It is to the hospitable people of Hopkins that I dedicate this story.

ILLUSTRATOR'S NOTE

Caribbean people have a story about cassava bread that they like to tell. When Christopher Columbus was preparing to sail home from the Americas to Spain, the native people of the Caribbean were very generous and filled the hulls of his ship with dried cassava loaves. During that first long and difficult voyage back, the Spaniards ran out of the regular food stocks they had brought. If not for the cassava bread, they would have perished on the seas.

To research the illustrations for this book, I traveled to the island of Dominica in the Lesser Antilles for a seventeen-day stay. Currently about 2,500 people live in the Carib Territory on the northeast end of the island.

Fortuitously, classes on basket weaving were held right under the guest house where I was staying (the house was constructed on stilts). I attended as many classes as I could. And, under the instruction of the master basket weaver Mr. Alphonse Frances, I completed my own cassava squeezer.

I am very grateful to Mr. Frances for his patience and his willingness to share his knowledge. I am also grateful to Chief Irvince Auguiste, to Parliamentary Representative Mr. François Barrie, to Mr. Napoleon Sanford and his lovely daughter Mauricia Sanford, and to my host at the guest house, Ms. Patsy Thomas.